THIS WALKER BOOK BELONGS TO:

First published in Great Britain 1976 by Hamish Hamilton Ltd
This edition published 2000 by Walker Books Ltd
87 Vauxhall Walk, London SE11 5HJ

2 4 6 8 10 9 7 5 3

© 1976, 2000 Anthony Browne

This book has been typeset in Gill Sans.

Printed in Hong Kong

British Library Cataloguing in Publication Data
A catalogue record for this book is available
from the British Library.

ISBN 0-7445-6772-6 (hb)
ISBN 0-7445-7707-1 (pb)

Through the Magic Mirror

Anthony Browne

WALKER BOOKS

AND SUBSIDIARIES

LONDON • BOSTON • SYDNEY

Toby sat in the big chair. He was fed up.
Fed up with books, fed up with toys,
fed up with everything.

He went into the living-room.
Nothing was happening there.

Going back upstairs he saw himself in a mirror.
Something looked very strange. What was wrong?

He put out his hand to touch the mirror –
and walked right through it!

He was out in the street.

It seemed like the same old street, but was it?

An invisible man passed by.

On the corner was an easel.
On the easel was a painting
of a painting
of a painting.

Just then a dog came along,
taking a man for a walk.

Toby walked on.
Two men were painting a fence.

Toby took another look.
He could hardly believe what he saw.

Suddenly the sky became dark as a flock of choirboys flew overhead.

A terrified cat darted past,
chased by a gang of hungry mice.

And the traffic seemed somehow different.

Across the road Toby saw a poster for the zoo.

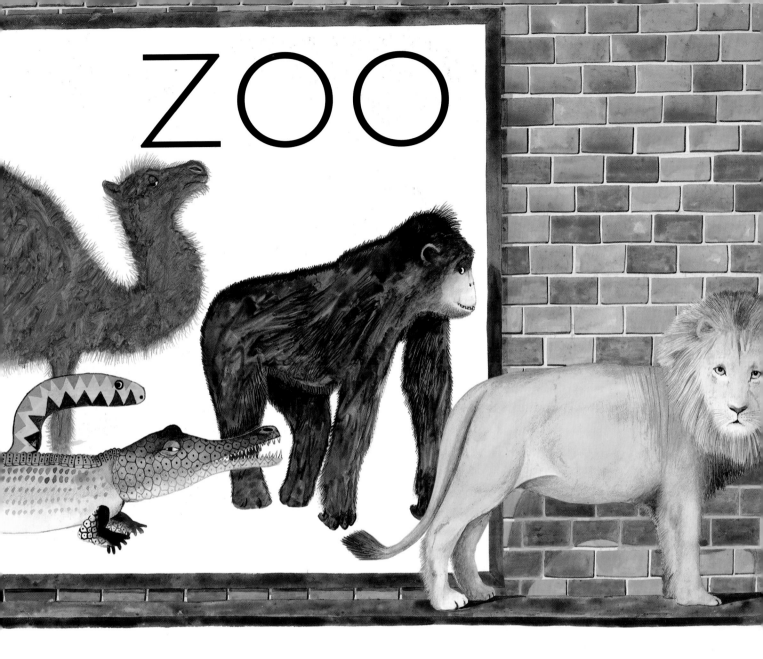

But what was happening?

Toby ran as fast as he could.
Where was that mirror?

Of course, there it was,
right behind him.

Toby stepped through, back into his own house.

He turned around and looked at himself in the mirror. When he saw his face, he smiled.

Then he ran
down to tea.